Paddington's Story Book Treasury

Michael Bond

Illustrated by John Lobban

Colour Library Direct

Contents

CLD 21319

This edition published in 1999 for Colour Library Direct, Godalming Business Centre,
Woolsack Way, Godalming, Surrey GU7 1XW .

1 3 5 7 9 10 8 6 4 2

ISBN: 1 84100 121 X

Printed and bound in China by Imago

Paddington
Bear

PADDINGTON

One day Mr and Mrs Brown were standing in
Paddington Station. They were waiting for their
daughter Judy who was coming home from school.
Suddenly Mr Brown noticed something small and
furry behind a pile of mailbags.

"Look over there," he said to Mrs Brown, "I'm
sure I saw a bear."

"A *bear*?" said Mrs Brown. "On Paddington Station? Don't be silly, Henry. There can't be."

But there was. It had a funny kind of hat and it was sitting all by itself on an old suitcase near the Lost Property Office.

As they drew near, the bear stood up and politely raised its hat. "Good afternoon," it said, in a small clear voice. "Can I help you?"

"We were wondering if *we* could help *you*,"

said Mrs Brown. "Where ever have you come from?"
The bear looked around carefully before
replying. "Darkest Peru. I stowed away and I lived
on marmalade!"

Mrs Brown spied a label round the bear's neck. It said simply:

"Henry," she exclaimed, "we shall have to take him home with us."

"But we don't even know his name," began Mr Brown.

"We'll call him Paddington," said Mrs Brown. "Because that's where we found him."

Mrs Brown went off to look for Judy and Mr Brown
took Paddington into the buffet for something to eat.

He left Paddington sitting at a corner table
near the window. He soon returned carrying two
steaming cups of tea and a large plate piled high
with sticky cakes.

After his long journey Paddington felt so hungry and thirsty he didn't know which to do first – eat or drink.

"I think I'll try both at the same time if you don't mind, Mr Brown," he announced. And without waiting for a reply he climbed up onto the table. Mr Brown stared out of the window, pretending he had tea with a bear at Paddington Station every day of his life.

When Mrs Brown came into the buffet with Judy
she threw up her hands in horror.

"Henry," she said. "What are you doing to that
poor bear? He's covered all over with cream and jam."

At the sound of Mrs Brown's voice Paddington
jumped so much he stepped on a patch of strawberry
jam and fell over backwards into his saucer of tea.

"I think we'd better go before anything else happens," said Mr Brown. And he quickly led the way out of the buffet.

Judy took Paddington's paw and squeezed it.

"Come along," she said. "We'll take you home in a taxi. Then you can have a nice hot bath and meet my brother Jonathan."

Paddington had never been in a taxi before. He found it very exciting and he stood on a little tip-up seat behind the driver so that he could wave to the people in the street.

Soon they pulled up outside a large house with a green front door.

When they were indoors Judy took Paddington up to
his room to unpack.

"I haven't got very much," said Paddington.
"Only some marmalade…

and my scrapbook…

…and a sort of South American penny."

He held up a photograph.
"And that is my
Aunt Lucy. She had
it taken just before
she went into the
Home for Retired Bears."

Next Judy showed Paddington to the bathroom.

As soon as he was on his own he turned on the taps and then climbed onto a stool in order to look out of the window.

Then he tried writing his name on the steamy glass with his paw. It took him rather a long time and when he looked round he found to his surprise that the bath was so full of water it was starting to run over the side.

He closed his eyes and, holding his nose with one paw, he jumped in.

The water was hot, soapy and very deep, and to his horror he found he couldn't get out. He couldn't even see to turn the taps off.

Paddington tried calling out "Help", at first in a quiet voice, so as not to disturb anyone and then much louder, "HELP! HELP!"

But still nobody came.

Then he had an idea.

He took off his hat and began using it to bale out the water.

Downstairs, Judy was telling her brother all about Paddington.

Suddenly, she felt a PLOP.

Looking up she saw a dark, wet patch on the ceiling.

"Paddington," she cried. "He must be in trouble. Quick!"

And together they raced out of the room.

Jonathan and Judy leant over the side of the
bath and lifted a dripping and very frightened
Paddington on to the floor.

"What a mess!" said Jonathan. "We'd better
wipe it up pretty quickly."

"Oh Paddington," said Judy. "What a good job we found you in time. You might have drowned."

Paddington sat up. "What a good job I had my hat," he said.

Some time later a beautifully clean Paddington
came downstairs. Settling himself down in a small
armchair by the fire, he put his paws behind his
head and stretched out his toes.

It was nice being a bear—especially a bear
called Paddington. He had a feeling that life with
the Browns was going to be fun.

Paddington goes Shopping

One day, not long after Paddington went to live with
the Browns at number thirty-two Windsor Gardens,
Mrs Brown thought she would take him out shopping.

"We're going to the Portobello Road," explained
Judy. "It's a big market quite near here."

"I should bring your pocket money," added
Jonathan. "There's a lot to see."

Paddington didn't need asking twice and soon afterwards they all set off.

Suddenly they turned a corner and he found himself in what seemed like a different world:

a world of shops and street barrows, gold and silver ornaments, books, old furniture, fruit and vegetables, people … his eyes grew larger and larger as he tried to take it all in.

One shop was even having its photograph taken.

"That's a new supermarket," explained Judy. "There must be something special on."

Paddington's mouth began to water as he peered through the glass. "Perhaps I could do some shopping for you, Mrs Brown?" he said hopefully.

Mrs Brown hesitated. She wasn't at all sure about letting him go off on his own quite so soon, but Jonathan told her not to worry.

"Even Paddington can't get lost in a supermarket," he said. "What goes in must come out."

"We can meet him by the cash desk on our way back," added Judy.

Paddington felt most important as he entered the shop.

He lifted his hat to the manager, who was standing just inside the door, and then consulted Mrs Brown's shopping list.

Everywhere he looked there were shelves piled high with packets and tins. There was even one shelf with nothing but marmalade, so he could quite see why it was called a *super*market.

His paws were soon full and he was just beginning
to wish he'd left his suitcase at home when he saw
the manager coming towards him pushing a large
basket on wheels.

"May I suggest you have one of these, Sir?"
he called.

"You can take as much as you want now," he continued.

"Can I really?" exclaimed Paddington.

The manager nodded. "Yes, we like to make our customers happy."

Paddington looked most impressed. "In that case," he said, "I think I'll have two baskets – just to make sure."

The more Paddington saw of the supermarket the more he liked it, and he felt sure Mrs Brown would be pleased when she saw all her free groceries.

The other customers looked on in amazement.

"Perhaps he's trying to win an eating prize," suggested one lady, as he went past, his baskets laden with goods.

But the customers weren't the only ones who were watching Paddington with interest.

Since he had been in the shop the manager had

been joined by several other important-looking men, and as he reached the cash desk one of them gave a signal, and they all started to clap.

Paddington had never been in a shop where they tried so hard to make their customers happy, and he gave the men a friendly wave as he unloaded his baskets.

"Well done!" said the lady, handing him a ticket. "I hope you've brought a lorry with you. There's over fifty pounds' worth here!"

Paddington stared at the long roll of paper in his paw.

"Over fifty pounds' worth!" he gasped, hardly able to believe his eyes or his ears.

Giving the man who had said he could take as much as he wanted one of his hardest ever stares, he opened his suitcase and peered inside.

"But I've only got three pence!"

Looking up, Paddington suddenly caught sight of a crowd of people coming towards him.

"Watch out!" cried the lady as he made a grab for his shopping.

But it was too late.

With a roar like an express train the whole lot
began to tumble down off the counter.

Paddington was still sitting on the floor covered with groceries when the Browns rushed into the shop to see what was going on.

All in all he decided he was much safer where he was for the time being.

"You wouldn't think," said the manager, "that giving someone a prize would be so difficult."

"A prize?" echoed the Browns. The manager pointed to a large notice on the wall.

"This young bear," he said, "happens to be our thousandth customer today. Perhaps you'd like to tell him he's won a free supply of groceries!"

"All of which," said Judy, as they staggered home laden with shopping, "only goes to show that bears always fall on their feet."

"Even in supermarkets!" agreed Jonathan.

Paddington sniffed the air happily. "I like the Portobello Road," he said. "I think I shall always do my shopping here from now on."

Paddington at the Seaside

"Today," said Mr Brown at breakfast one bright, summer morning, "feels like the kind of day for taking a young bear to the seaside. Hands up all those who agree."

Jonathan, Judy and Mrs Brown all put up their
hands. And Paddington raised both of his paws as
well, just to make sure.

Everyone was very excited, and by the time they set out the Browns' car was so full of things there was hardly room to move.

Paddington carefully fastened his safety belt, and then peered out of the window as he felt the car turn a corner.

"Are we nearly there, Mr Brown?" he asked hopefully.

Mr Brown removed a spade handle from his left ear. "I'm afraid not," he said gloomily. "We've only just left Windsor Gardens, and it's a very long way to the sea."

Mr Brown was right. It *was* a long journey. But when they reached the seaside the sight of the sand and the water soon made up for it.

Paddington gave an excited sniff as he climbed out of the car. Even the air had a different smell.

"That's because it's special seaside air," said Mrs Brown. "It's very good for you."

Paddington looked round anxiously as Mr Brown began laying out the beach things.

"I hope all the air doesn't get used up, Mrs Brown," he said in a loud voice. And he gave a man who was doing some deep-breathing exercises a very hard stare indeed.

"Come on, Paddington," called Judy. "Let's go for a swim."

It took Paddington some while to get ready. He wasn't the sort of bear who believed in taking chances and by the time he went in the sea he was wearing so many things he promptly sank.

"No wonder!" cried Judy, as she went to his rescue. "You haven't even bothered to blow up your paw-bands!"

"Fancy wearing a duffle-coat!" exclaimed Jonathan.

"I thought the water might be cold," gasped Paddington.

After his paw-bands had been properly blown up
Paddington went in the water again, and with some
help from Jonathan and Judy he was soon
swimming very well indeed.

After his swim Paddington settled down in a deckchair in order to dry out.

He had hardly closed his eyes when he heard something very strange going on behind him.

First there was a loud cry.

Then there was the sound of people booing.

"They're watching Mr Briggs' Punch and Judy," explained Mrs Brown.

Paddington jumped up and looked at the others as if
he could hardly believe his ears. But Mr and Mrs
Brown seemed much too busy with the picnic things
to be bothered, so he turned and hurried up the
beach towards the spot where the noise was
coming from.

"Where's Paddington?" asked Jonathan, when he and Judy arrived back shortly afterwards carrying some ice creams.

"I hope he won't be long," said Judy. "I've got him a special giant cone. He'll be most upset if it all melts."

Jonathan glanced up and down the beach. "Crikey!" he said suddenly. "Look over there!"

The Browns gave a gasp as they turned to follow the
direction of Jonathan's gaze.

Something very odd seemed to be going on inside the Punch and Judy tent.

There was a large bulge in one side and it was heaving up and down almost as if it was alive.

Suddenly the tent began moving across the sand, scattering people in all directions. It just missed a large sand castle, went twice round the ice cream man and then headed towards the sea.

"Quick!" shouted Judy. "Let's cut it off!"

But she was too late.

"Paddington!" cried Judy, as a familiar figure swam into view. "What on earth are you doing? That's the second time I've had to rescue you!"

Paddington stared at her in amazement. "But I
went to rescue *you*!" he exclaimed. "Mrs Brown said
you were being punched by Mr Briggs."

Mrs Brown looked at Paddington in astonishment.
Then her face cleared.

"I didn't say Mr Briggs was *punching* Judy," she
explained. "I said it was his Punch *and* Judy."

"It's a puppet theatre," said Judy. "They often
have them at the seaside. There's one puppet called
Mr Punch, and when he gets cross all the audience
have to boo."

If it took the Browns a long time to explain a Punch and Judy show to Paddington, it took them even longer to explain Paddington to Mr Briggs.

But when he saw the enormous crowd watching them from the promenade his face lit up. It was the biggest audience he'd had for a long time and he decided to make the most of it and put another show on there and then.

"You can have a seat in the front row," he said to Paddington. "I expect bears do very good boos."

One way and another Paddington enjoyed his day out at the seaside. But all good things come to an end, and when it was time to leave he stood for a moment holding up an empty marmalade jar.

"I'm just collecting some sea air for the journey home," he announced.

"I think I shall sleep so well on the way back I may lose all of today's air with my snores!"

Paddington's Garden

One day Paddington decided to make a list of all the nice things there were about being a bear and living with the Browns at number thirty-two Windsor Gardens.

It was a long list and he had almost reached the end of the paper when he suddenly realised he'd left out one of the nicest things of all... the garden itself!

Paddington liked the Browns' garden. It was quiet
and peaceful, and there were times when it might
not have been in London at all.

But nice gardens usually mean a lot of hard
work, and after a day at his office Mr Brown often
wished it wasn't quite so large.

It was Mrs Brown who first thought of giving Jonathan, Judy and Paddington a piece each of their own.

"It will keep them out of mischief," she said.

"And it will help you at the same time."

So Mr Brown marked out three squares, and to make it more exciting he said he would give a prize to whoever had the best idea.

Early next morning all three set to work.

Judy thought she would grow some flowers, and Jonathan started to make a paved garden, but Paddington didn't know what to do.

Gardening was much harder than it looked – especially with paws, and he soon grew tired of digging.

In the end he decided to do some shopping.

He had some savings left over from his pocket
money and he bought a wheelbarrow, a trug,
a trowel, and a large packet of assorted seeds.

It seemed very good value indeed – especially as
he still had two pence left over.

The shopkeeper told him that when planning a new garden it was a good idea to stand some way away first, in order to picture what it would look like when it was finished. So, taking a jar of his best chunky marmalade, Paddington set out to visit the nearby building site.

By the time he got there it was the middle of the
morning, and as the men were all at their tea break
he sat down on a pile of bricks, put the jar of
marmalade on a wooden platform for safety, and
then peered hopefully towards the Browns' garden.

BEST MARMALADE

After sitting there for some while without getting a single idea Paddington decided to try taking a short walk instead.

When he got back his eyes nearly popped out.

A man was emptying the concrete mixer on the very spot where he'd left his jar of chunky marmalade.

At that moment the foreman came round the corner and seeing the look on Paddington's face he stopped to ask what was wrong.

Paddington pointed to the pile of wet cement.

"All my chunks have been buried!" he exclaimed hotly.

The foreman called his men together. "There's a
young bear gentleman here who's lost some very
valuable chunks," he said urgently.

They set to work clearing the cement.

Soon the ground was covered with small piles, but still there was no sign of Paddington's jar.

Suddenly there was a whirring sound from somewhere overhead and to Paddington's surprise a platform landed at his feet.

"My marmalade!" he exclaimed thankfully.

"Your marmalade?" echoed the foreman, staring at the jar. "Did you say marmalade?"

"That's right," said Paddington. "I put it there ready for my elevenses. It must have been taken up by mistake."

It was the foreman's turn to look as if he could
hardly believe his eyes.

"That's special quick-drying cement!" he wailed.
"It's probably going rock-hard already—ruined by a

bear's marmalade! No one will give me two pence for it now!"

Paddington opened his suitcase and felt in the secret compartment. "I will," he said eagerly.

123

Paddington took the lumps of concrete home in his
wheelbarrow and worked hard in his garden for the
rest of the day. When the builders saw the rockery
he had made with the concrete they were most
impressed and gave Paddington several plants to
finish it off for the time being…

...until his seeds started to grow.

Paddington's rockery fitted in so well with
Jonathan's paved garden and Judy's flower bed it
looked as though the whole thing had been planned.

Mr Brown was so pleased he decided to give them all an extra week's pocket money, and that afternoon they celebrated by having tea in the new garden.

After it was over Paddington stayed on for a while in order to finish off his list of all the nice things there were about being a bear and living at number thirty-two Windsor Gardens.

He had one more important item to add.

MY ROCKERY

Then he signed his name and added his special paw print...

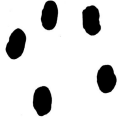

...just to show it was genuine.